THIS TIME AROUND
A CANADIAN WEREWOLF STORY

MARK LESLIE

Stark Publishing

STARK
PUBLISHING

Stark Publishing
Waterloo, ON
www.markleslie.ca

Publisher's Note: This is a work of fiction. Names, characters, places, and incidents are a product of the author's imagination. Real locales and public and celebrity names are sometimes used for atmospheric purposes. Any resemblance to actual people, living or dead, or to businesses, companies, events, institutions, or locales is either completely coincidental or is used in a completely fictional manner.

Book Layout © 2014 BookDesignTemplates.com
Cover Design © 2020 Juan Padron

This Time Around / Mark Leslie. -- 1st ed.
Hardcover ISBN: 978-1-989351-21-5
Trade Paperback Print ISBN: 978-1-989351-18-5
eBook ISBN: 978-1-989351-19-2
Audiobook ISBN: 978-1-989351-20-8

First paperback printing August 2020

For Sean Costello, who read this story and said:
"This is great. What happens next?"

Table of Contents

THIS TIME AROUND

Thursday August 14, 2014

6:04 AM

This time I woke to find myself sprawled naked in the grass, my shoulder nestled in a shrub and the coppery aftertaste of blood in my mouth. It was a cool morning, but humid, the unmistakable scent of the Hudson River hanging in the air.

I pulled my aching body into a sitting position and checked it over for injuries. Apart from the usual scrapes and scratches there was a nasty looking wound in my thigh. It hurt like it was no more than a bad bruise, but it looked like a bullet hole. I ran my hand down the leg and stuck my finger inside. Yes indeed, it was a bullet hole - the bullet was nestled just about an inch deep.

At least the bullet wasn't silver - now *that* I would have felt.

So to sum up my situation, there was a distinct taste of blood in my mouth and a bullet wound in my leg.

What the hell had I done this time?

I took a look around me. The park I was in was on the Hudson; that I could tell from the scent of the water. The early morning mist revealed beautiful Lady Liberty to me in teasing glimpses. Okay, so this was Battery Park. I was on the south western tip of Manhattan Island. And since I was currently a guest at the Algonquin Hotel in Mid-

Town, getting three quarters of the way across this island bare naked was going to be one hell of a chore.

Uncovering the mystery of what exactly I'd been up to during last night's full moon, would, of course, be another.

But I was a mystery writer after all; and was usually able to piece it all together upon examination of the evidence. My memories as a wolf were scattered and non-linear snatches of smells, sounds, tastes, feelings and sights, not often available to my human conscious mind. Trying to piece them together in my conscious mind often gave me a migraine. I'd always thought perhaps that was how I'd preserved my sanity.

Unfortunately, with my growing popularity as a mystery writer, it was becoming easier for people to recognize me - at least in human form, that is. Finding a picture of myself scampering about the city butt naked on the cover of the tabloids was not a pleasant thought.

Was it time to move out of New York?

No, after all, growing up reading Spider-Man comic books, I'd always wanted to live here. So I was living my childhood dream. In my dreams, though, I'd been the wall-crawler, swinging around the city rooftops and nabbing the bad guys - I'd never dreamed that I would be one of the monsters that Spider-Man often faced down, like that astronaut who, wearing a moon rock on a chain around his neck was afflicted with the curse of the were-wolf - something to do with wolves and the moon, I guess. But other than the concept of a full moon and werewolves, it never made sense to me. After all, every-one knows that being bitten by a werewolf is the way that a person becomes inflicted with the curse.

For me, it was a chance encounter with a wolf on a camping/hitchhiking trip through Upstate New York that led to my lycanthropic affliction.

The wolf had leapt from the bushes at the side of the highway just as a car came around the distant bend. With a failed attempt to abort the attack in mid-leap, its teeth nipped at my upraised right arm as it landed on me, the teeth barely sinking below the surface of my flesh. I fell back onto the road with the weight of the wolf hitting me on the chest, and the wolf quickly bounced off me and across the highway, rather than tear out my throat in one single gesture. I'd later learned that wolves do not kill for sport, but for food and for territory. The attack on me must have been an attempt at food that night, because if the goal had been to just kill me, it would have been over. The goal to consume me wasn't something the wolf could do with the car approaching, so it simply aborted the at-tack and ran - likely on to find a bird, rabbit or squirrel.

The driver, of course, didn't see the wolf attack, just that I'd been lying on the highway. He picked me up, a salesman eager to have someone to talk to - his incidental saving of my life was nothing more than a fortunate side-effect of his finding a driving companion. After hearing me tell him about the wolf attack that had nearly taken my life, he made the comment "pretty scary" and then regaled me with tales of his travels, facts about the Em-pire State and his goals for retirement.

Because we were heading in the same direction and he was thirsty for company, I ended up bunking with him at the hotel when he stayed for the night, he being eager to have me sleep in the chair in his own hotel room as his conversational prostitute.

And I'd ended up riding with him all the way in to New York City.

I'd stayed with him again upon our arrival into the city, engaging in another marathon conversation session in his hotel room. And, although he was a little peculiar, I couldn't help but like this man, not only because he'd accidentally saved my life, but also because of the incredible knowledge he would disperse, all with the innocence and wondrous thirst of a child.

Fortunately, he also knew the city well, so it was a good initiation to the city for me to spend my first night there with him.

Actually, Buddy (that's his name) and I became friends, and he visits me every time he returns to the city, usually for dinner, some drinks, and long conversations - the one-sided kind he is so enamored with - well into the wee hours of the night.

And, although Buddy never really asked me all that much about me and my personal life, he remembered how we'd met during the wolf attack. So, he often greeted me with the nickname "Wolfman" never knowing how close he really was to the truth.

I'd been in the city for almost three weeks before my first experience of lycanthropy. After getting over the fact of understanding what had happened to me and the reality of living with it, I found it desperately hard to hold a job. Sure, I wanted to be a writer - but I had to secure some sort of job to keep an income. And holding the types of jobs I was skilled for, being a waiter or a delivery driver, was often difficult. Waking up naked far from home usually left me late for work. Never-mind the times that I'd destroyed my uniform when turning into a wolf before I had the chance to get home and undress. And trying to avoid the night shift for several days in a row every month by calling in sick often left my employer with another good reason to fire me.

It wasn't until I was about six months into my curse that I'd discovered I could put my wolf-blood to good use. Since becoming a werewolf, my human self retained some of the benefits of my wolfish nature. My senses were all heightened - I no longer needed to wear glasses, for example - and my strength had seemed to double, sometimes quadruple, depending on the proximity of the full-moon.

My ability to heal also dramatically improved and my constitution has never been better. I haven't had a cold or caught a flu virus since becoming a werewolf.

So while it's not a glamorous life, it's not all entirely bad.

My extra strength and immune system allowed me to work the more dangerous labor jobs that paid well and most people couldn't stay at long. Then, later, once building more of a nest egg, I was able move up within the companies I worked for, by being able to see and hear things that normal people missed out on. In essence, my EQ and ability to interact with and influence people was dramatically improved. I was able to pull off this incredible charisma.

It's how I was able to get an editor to agree to read my first novel.

Along those same lines, the heightened senses allowed me to more properly explore the senses when writing descriptions in a novel, thus improving my writing style and ability to draw readers right into the scene.

It's probably why I was such a successful mystery writer.

With the success came appearances on talk shows and the occasional red carpet type of event, such as when one of my novels had been turned into a feature film. Recognition came with that success, making it harder for me to simply blend into the crowd.

Yes, even in New York, where the extraordinary seemed commonplace, it was hard for a naked celebrity to just blend into the scenery.

Not that I wasn't used to having to find new ways to sneak back home naked after a night of howling at the moon, but the celebrity aspect was starting to make the task of not being recognized that much more difficult.

After quickly determining that there were no humans nearby in the narrow sliver of park I was in, I decided to take the time to remove the bullet from my leg. If I didn't it would be lodged inside. The bleeding had already stopped and the wound had already started to heal, so I could tell it was at least a few hours old. By the end of the day, the healing, I knew, would be well advanced, and by the day after the next the scab might even by ready to fall off. Not that I often let the scabs fall off on their own. I relished picking at them.

I was able to pry the wound open enough to snag the bullet fragment between the tip of my index finger and my thumbnail. After a minute or so of twisting and prying, it slipped right out.

I couldn't very well walk around with a bullet lodged in my thigh. The thought of setting off metal detectors, now almost as common as pay phones used to be, wasn't all that appealing to me.

Getting up, I flung the bullet fragment into the murky depths of the Hudson.

It was now time to make my way back home.

Judging by the sun's position in the sky and the sounds of traffic, it was likely some time after 5:30 AM. The sun had just come up maybe ten or fifteen minutes ago, but it being an August morning, the humidity and smog hung in the air like a light morning fog.

The first significant set of commuters would likely be arriving on the 6:20 AM Staten Island Ferry. The Ferry landed just south of where I was now. If I were able to find at least some of the right clothes, I could perhaps blend in with those folks and make my way to the subway. Provided I could get a handful of change I'd be able to take the subway. If not, I had a long walk ahead of me. And, despite my healing ability and the slightly thicker padding on my feet now, walking that many miles in my bare feet on pavement and concrete still wasn't pleasant.

I paused to survey the park in a little more detail and pick up on the scents around me, at least the ones that weren't the usual typical background scents here, such as the grass, the sap from the trees and the cigarette butts. There was the smell of semen mingled with latex, from a condom that I could see now that I'd sensed it, about three yards to my right, just beneath a park bench. Near it I could see a newspaper, smell the newsprint, the stale remnants of cheap cologne, the smell of vaginal juices and the bitter dregs left behind in a coffee cup lying on its side. But I could smell another distinct vaginal scent that wasn't obscured by latex coming from the vicinity. I started walking in that direction.

On the other side of a tree near the bench, and out of the line of sight from where I'd originally stood, there was a pair of pink panties. That's where the vaginal juice smell was coming from. I headed over and picked the panties up, judging whether or not I'd be able to fit into them.

It's amazing what people throw away and in what places. While the origin of these panties seemed obvious to me based on the other evidence - a pair of lovers had likely enjoyed each other in the dark on this bench - I'd always wondered, for example, why you sometimes see a single shoe on the side of the highway or on the side of a road. Who throws out such articles of clothing and why there? I'd never met anyone in all my travels who admitted to losing or throwing away a single shoe while in a vehicle or traveling - so why, in all my time, was it such a common sight?

A mystery to solve another day I thought as I bent over, muttered "Desperate time," and stepped into the panties and pulled them up my legs.

Fortunately they had a good bit of play in them, so, though snug, I was able to pull them on.

It was a start at least.

I kept walking in that same direction, feeling I was on a roll.

Maybe I'd even find a pair of shoes in my size. Perhaps a nice set of cherry red pumps with stiletto heels.

As I was walking, a snippet of memory from last night came to me. *The squeal of tires and brakes and a bright, painful flash of headlight beams.* The sudden memory burst stopped me in my tracks. The memory flashed through my mind again, this time *the smell of rubber burning, overtop of a stronger background fishy smell*, then the memory was gone again. I pawed at it tentatively, but couldn't bring anything else back.

Instead I started thinking about the last memory I had as a human last night.

I was staying at the Algonquin Hotel. Ever since that one novel of mine was made into a blockbuster movie two and a half years ago, the rest of my novels had been republished and the royalties started screaming in. With the advance from the movie rights having been socked away into a secure investment, and with all the extra cash coming in, I finally abandoned my Chelsea bachelor apartment, and decided to take up residence at the Algonquin Hotel.

The Algonquin, of course, known for its literary history.

If I could live out my childhood dream of living in New York and being a writer like Stan Lee, the genius who'd created Spider-Man, I could live out a later adult fantasy in which I was a writer-in-residence of sorts at this spot.

The management was able to cut me enough of a deal for the long-term room, and I made frequent appearances within the lobby, where the cultural elite liked to hang out before Broadway shows or the Opera. I didn't mind hanging out there myself, and it was a thrill to be part of the ambiance. After all, it was the ambiance of the lobby area of the Algonquin that had attracted me in the first place.

So last night, after a productive writing session, I'd headed out for an early evening stroll. I thought I would have enough time to get to Central Park, where I often liked to be before a change. Being locked up in a hotel room as a wolf wasn't a good thing, not if you wanted to stay in the good books with hotel management. Besides, I liked to also ensure that I gave my other-half a good outing, the ability to run and expend all that pent-up energy in a healthy way.

When I was planning on doing a Central Park outing, I often stashed clothes nearby in the park for when I awoke. I had to, of course, keep finding new places to stash my clothes because of the times when I returned to find my clothes missing. It's amazing at how quickly certain homeless folks can be at finding things you would have thought were well hidden.

By then, of course, I'd stopped having to also stash a set of keys or a wallet or I.D. or anything like that. One of the benefits of living at the Algonquin was that the Concierge knew me and I could get in and up to my room without any hassle whenever I didn't have my key or I.D.

Last night, however, I don't remember even making it to Central Park.

It was evening, the sun was setting. I'd left the Algonquin wearing a pair of disposable clothes and with my extra change of clothes stashed in a plastic grocery bag - no, I didn't like to get naked before the change and thus save the clothes I was in - so, I wore either older or cheap discount store clothing on "change" nights.

I was walking up 5th Avenue towards the park ...

... and that's where my human memory fails. The wolf-related amnesia I suffered from typically struck anywhere from five to fifteen minutes before and after a transition. That told me it's possible I didn't even make it to Central Park before I changed.

The other clue I had was the fact that, when I made the change in Central Park, my wolf-self very often didn't leave the boundaries of the park. With plenty of places to run, cavort and hunt down prey of the rodent and other small animal variety, there was little reason for my wolf-self to leave the park.

Consumed in the memories and the attempt at regurgitating the events of last night, I almost failed to detect the scent of another human just downwind to my right. It was a single person, a man, and his scent was coming from around the corner of the building on State Street where the people from the Staten Island ferry came in - the scent was getting stronger as he approached.

I glanced down at myself, clad in the flimsy and tight pink panties, then to the left and right. There was no place for me to hide. It was too late to duck under cover.

I could only hope that this person wasn't one of my fans.

Based on the unfamiliar scent, I knew this was a person I hadn't met before - that was something at least. There was also the slight tinge of ammonia or a similar cleaning agent on this person, so my initial thought was that this might be one of the cleaners leaving the Wall Street office towers after a busy night of work.

He stopped as I rounded the corner, and there he stood, about five and a half feet tall. He had a large round face, receding hairline and a few untendered wisps of long, unshaven hair on his lower chin. His eyes were almond shaped and a very bright blue. He wore a red plaid shirt and bright yellow suspenders to hold up his brown pleated slacks. Over that he wore a thin windbreaker jacket. On his feet he wore these long red sneakers, and his stance was such that his feet were angled outwards, the way you sometimes see a clown standing.

He smiled at me. A huge, unabashed full tooth smile and said in a loud and deep voice, not unlike one a game show announcer might use to call the next contestant on stage from the audience. "Lovely morning, isn't it!"

Not one double-take for the way I was dressed.

Yeah, I know, I know, this is New York after all. But still, you'd expect at least a slight pause. And, even in the average New Yorker used to seeing the strange relatively regularly, I would expect to smell at least the slightest twinge of fear. After all, a strange man in a pair of tight pink panties wandering the streets typically signaled that something was amiss.

Before I could say anything, he asked: "Do you happen to have the time?" He said this in the same loud announcer-type voice. It was obviously a planned and well-practiced line.

I instinctively glanced at my bare wrist and then took another look at him. He was wearing a watch.

Then I understood. It explained the well-rehearsed line, which was a little conversation starter, something it was okay for one stranger to ask of another. This poor guy was a little slow. But he certainly wasn't living on the street - he had a clean, recently bathed smell to him. My instincts kicked in, knowing he was a person who required adult supervision, protection. So, either he was lost, having wandered out of a protected area, or his supervisory support was nearby. I knew the second option couldn't be right, because I would have smelled another person in the vicinity. And I could tell that he and I were the only people outside within about a one block radius.

"I'm sorry," I told him. "I don't have the time, but I think I can guess."

His eyes lit up. This was going to be a game of sorts. He raised his wrist and looked at his own watch. "Okay, then you guess. And I'll tell you if you're right. I'm Wally."

"Hi Wally. I'm Michael. So, Wally, if I guess correctly, what sort of prize is that worth?"

"Prize?" he asked. Again, he wasn't trepidatious in the slightest. His scent revealed playfulness and wonder.

"Yeah," I said. "I'm a little short of clothes here. Maybe you could help by lending me some clothing if I guess correctly. Like, maybe your jacket."

Immediately fear fused out of him. But he didn't step back. He wasn't afraid of me, but of something else. A consequence of the thought of giving away his clothes? "No," he said quietly. "Can't do that. Can't do that. Ma says that I need to keep track of my things, like my clothes. Have to keep track of them. Can't do that."

"Okay, okay, maybe you could help me find some clothes."

The fear was immediately replaced with the playfulness again, and deeper excitement. "Okay," he nodded.

"Speaking of your Ma, Wally, where is she?"

His scent got frightened again, but also worried and concerned and confused. "She's on the ferry. I stopped to tie my shoes and watched an ant walking right through all the people. Then I caught up with Ma again, but I started to worry about the ant. I ran back to him, to make sure nobody had stepped on him. I didn't hear the ferry man announce the gate was closing. I couldn't find the ant, but I kept looking. Then Ma was calling for me, and the ferry was leaving. So I'm waiting here for Ma. I still can't find the ant, so I started walking to find him. I saw other ants, but not the one I had seen before. Still can't find him."

"It's okay, Wally. I'm sure that the ant is okay. And your Ma saw you on the dock, didn't she?"

"Yes. She was calling to me."

"She's probably going to be on the next ferry."

"You think so?"

"Of course," and then my nurturing instinct kicked in slightly higher. It suddenly seemed likely to me that Wally's mother was a cleaning lady with neither the family support nor the money to afford someone to look after her son while she worked. So she likely did what she had to - adhere him to the same schedule as her, working throughout the night and sleeping in the morning.

"And I'll stay here with you until she does." Of course, it would certainly be tricky for me to not be seen by anybody dressed the way I was, but I'd deal with that when the time came.

"Okay," he said. "But do we still get to find some clothes for you?"

"Sure," I smiled. Then I caught the scent of someone approaching from what seemed to be South Street. It was a man, not quite as clean smelling as Wally, but not so unwashed as to be a street person. Also, he wasn't wearing cologne or after shave, so it wasn't likely a business person.

"Wally, listen," I said. "Someone is coming. And I'm … a little shy about people not seeing me dressed the way I am. So I'm just going to hide. I'll still be nearby, though, okay."

"Okay," he said.

Just a few yards to the west there was a series of concrete barricades, due to construction that was going on with the pier and docking station. I quickly bounded in that direction, easily leapt over the barricade and ducked down behind it.

As I'd ducked down, I was struck with another memory from my last stint as a wolf. This time it was the deafening roar of a gunshot and the unmistakable smell of gunpowder; a flash of pain in my leg and somewhere, muffled, in the background a child-like voice that said something like: "No, not the nice doggie!"

I shook my head - now wasn't the time to have a flash-back - and focused on Wally and the approaching stranger.

The footsteps got closer as the scent became stronger.

"Well, what do we have here?" a voice called out. It was deeper in tone than Wally's and spoken in a loud, carefully pronounced way. The accent was different in pitch, not the same New York/Brooklyn flavor of speech common to this area, but more like my own accent, which had a New England ring to it.

"Good morning." Wally said, and then, in his announcer voice said: "Would you happen to have the time?"

"The time?" the stranger responded in a sneering tone. "You're the one wearing a watch, dude." There was a pause. "Oh, I get it, you're a retard."

"My Ma says that it's not nice to use that word." Again, Wally's scent wasn't fearful, it was indignant, offended.

"Well your Ma isn't here to stop me, now, is she bub?"

"Uh, no, my Ma is on the ferry."

"I see." There was another pause. "Okay, man, give me your watch."

"Oh no." The fear became obvious this time not only in Wally's scent but in the way his voice broke when he continued to speak. "Can't do that. Ma says that I need to keep track of my things, like my clothes and my watch."

I stood up at that point. The stranger was facing away from me. He was about my height, wearing faded jeans and a crew-cut t-shirt. He had long greasy blond hair that covered the sides of his face. Wally didn't notice that I'd moved. His eyes never left the man in front of him. I quickly stepped onto the barricade and down onto the other side then strode quietly towards the two.

"I don't give a rat's ass what your Ma says." The stranger said, his finger jabbing at Wally's chest as he leaned in closer to my friend. "I said 'hand over that watch.' And let me see your wallet while we're at it." I was just a few steps away and gaining ground quickly.

"Can't do that." Wally said, his heart racing. "Can't do that. Can't do that. Can't do that."

The stranger grabbed Wally's wrist and pulled him closer, his angle changing enough that he spotted me from the corner of his eye.

His head turned in my direction. "What the hell do you want?" he said, his scent revealing a slight bit of fear, and then, after a brief double take in seeing the way I was dressed, he melted into a grin, his scent reeked of confidence and in the same sneering voice he'd used before, said: "Oh, another retard. But it looks like someone already got your stuff. Nice panties, dude!" He started laughing.

"I'll give you one warning," I said in a calm and quiet voice. "Leave him alone or you'll regret it."

As I spoke the words, the man's confidence started to waver. He immediately maneuvered behind Wally, taking Wally's right arm and bending it up against his back. Wally's face gave off a look of pain that I could smell off of him too. That really bothered me.

"Back off buddy," he said, his free hand coming up with a knife. He pressed the blade against Wally's throat.

"Michael, help me," Wally said. "Can't get blood on my clothes. Can't. Ma will be upset and think I can't take care of my things."

"Shut up!" the stranger said

It was the split second he was distracted when I made my move. One hand going for his throat, the other for the hand holding the knife. He didn't stand a chance. By the time he noticed I'd moved, I'd already had a firm grip on his throat with my left hand while I knocked the knife out of his left mitt with my right.

After disarming him, I thrust my right hand up and with a quick palm jab, broke his nose.

He stumbled back a couple of steps, blood gushing from his nose.

I moved forward and gave his chest a push. He fell back on his ass, his hands furtively trying to stop the blood pumping from his nostrils, his eyes wide - he looked more like a kid that had been eating from a bowl of strawberries and got caught, his lips and cheeks coated in red and these wide "oh shit" eyes.

I let out a low, deep laugh which was part growl.

That's when the confusion I smelled off him turned to an ice cold fear.

Behind me, Wally's scent still revealed fear.

"Oh no, Michael. He's got blood all over his shirt. His Ma is going to be upset now."

"That's okay," I told Wally as I reached down and grabbed this guy by the hair. "His Ma knows that he's a bad boy."

He didn't resist me, he just whined and held onto my hand as I lifted him off of the ground and put him down on the other side of me. I gave him a quick kick with the side of my foot, knocking the wind out of him, and whispered for him not to struggle if he knew what was good for him.

I started walking in the direction of Battery Park, dragging this would-be mugger behind me by lifting him into the air and setting him down hard, almost as if he were a short, fetal-like walking stick. He let out a forced puff of air each time he connected with the ground. "I'll be right back, Wally," I called out over my shoulder.

I carry-dragged the man to the first set of bushes and told him to take his own clothes off.

"L-leave me alone. Please don't rape me," he whim-pered, and then for good measure, because he had to ensure I knew he was a tough guy. "Y-you f-fag."

"I'm not going to rape you, you little freak. Just take your shirt and pants off. I need your clothes, you dipshit. And you need to be taught a lesson."

A few minutes later, I emerged from the bush with this guy over my shoulder. His pants fit me okay, but his shirt was too bloody to wear. I'd torn it into strips and used a few of them to tie his hands behind his back. It had been nice to discard those panties finally, but I let him keep his underwear, which he was still wearing. I had stuffed the panties into his mouth to keep him from yelling out and secured it into place with another strip of his shirt.

Closer to a bus stop on State Street, where he was sure to be visible to thousands of morning commuters within the next hour, I tied this fellow, standing, to the post, and, using his own fresh blood wrote "BULLY" on his chest. Before I left I told him I'd be watching him and if he ever tried to take advantage of someone like he had this morn-ing, I'd show up out of nowhere and hurt and humiliate him in more ways than he could imagine.

The distinct smell of fresh urine overpowered the strong scent of his latest wave of fear.

Wally walked over to me, studying the writing on this thug's chest but ensuring he didn't get too close. His head twisted to the side, I could tell that he couldn't make out the writing.

"Are you okay, Wally?" I asked.

"Ayuh," Wally said, still distracted by this stranger. "Michael, he's a bad man, isn't he?"

"He sure is. But we don't need to worry about him any more, Wally. C'mon, let's go wait for your Mom to get back."

"Okay,"

On our walk over we could see the next ferry coming in, about 100 yards off shore. I fell into place behind Wally and studied the scent coming off of him. Mingled with his own scent and the ammonia was another person's. Similar, but tinged with a feminine perfume. It was his mother's scent, subtle, but there - as if she'd given him a tight hug in the space of the last couple of hours.

I walked as close to the end of the dock as I could and waited for the wind to shift. Mingled with the scent of the sea water, the fumes from the ferry and the multiple passengers, I couldn't pick up Wally's mother's scent, but I could detect that ammonia smell.

I turned to my friend. "She's on this ferry, Wally."

"She is?"

"Yes, she'll be docking in a few minutes. I'm going to leave you now. You stay here, okay."

"Okay." His eyes turned sad and he gave off the scent of disappointment. "Do you have to go, Michael?"

"I do, Wally. I have some place I need to be."

"Okay," he stepped toward me and gave me a big hug. "G'bye, Michael."

I gently chuckled at his honest outward show of affection - how rare a thing between men in today's society.

The world needs more people like Wally. "Goodbye, my friend."

I turned and walked away, keeping track of him easily enough due to the shift in wind. When I'd walked about half a block, I turned to see that the ferry was docking. I could hear a woman's voice calling out to Wally and Wally responding. I felt assured that he was safely out of harm's way.

I quickened my pace, and started walking up State Street.

I needed to get more distance covered before rush hour, when the chance of being spotted became more of a threat. Well, at least I had pants now. And it was a summer day, not all that outrageous to be walking around without a shirt on.

But still.

When walking up Broadway, near Liberty Street I was overwhelmed with a flood of sensory memory. I know that it has been a dozen years since the tragic events of September 11th, 2001, but I swear I can still smell and taste the acrid smell of electrical fire, the jet fuel, the ash consisting of burnt flesh, concrete, paper, wood plastics and asbestos that I smelled in the days, weeks and months following the disaster. It was several years before I was able to approach this area from within about 10 blocks without being overcome with not just the smell and taste in the air, but with the horrific memories that went with each sensation.

Even now, though I swear I can still detect subtle hints of those scents and tastes in the air, I'm sure it's my mind that conjures it all back to full power. However, even now, there is no mistaking the very clear smell of utter despair that lingers in the air. Even years later, there continue to be an endless parade of tourists and visitors to the city who seek out the infamous landmark of Ground Zero; and they feed the area with this lasting olfactory image that constantly threatens to burn itself into my very psyche like a image burned onto a cathode ray tube.

Needless to say, I was glad to move past that tragic landmark.

I'd made it about three blocks north when the morning rush hour traffic started to really take form. That's when I remembered my appointment with Mack Halpin. Mack was my literary agent, a tough old codger who always had a cigar hanging out of the side of his mouth (recently more unlit than lit due to the city smoking by-laws) and an insulting quip at the ready.

Mack was a guy with a crusty surface and a good heart. He was a tough negotiation scrapper, and I was always glad he was fighting on my side. I'd be afraid to face him down even as a wolf.

One thing I didn't ever want to do, however, was piss Mack off for no reason. He was a punctual man who lived by a certain sense of old fashioned honor and principles such as "a man always honors his commitments" and "a man is only as good as his weakest words" - they always reminded me of the moral that Spider-Man learned in his very first adventure, that *with great power comes great responsibility*. God bless Stan Lee for delivering such basic wisdom in a format that could be easily digested by my young mind and yet continue to guide me throughout my adult life.

In any case, Mack and I had a breakfast appointment, and seeing a few folks in their business and power suits hustling into and out of cabs and office tower entrances, reminded me of Mack and the fact that we were supposed to be meeting in about an hour at the Metro Market just one street up from The Algonquin.

Considering where I was and the time I had to get home and change, I wasn't panicked; but I was realistically concerned. I mean, hoofing it by foot all the way was no longer an option unless I started running at top speed now and ran the entire distance. It could be done, but it would be very obvious - I mean, a man in jogging shorts, running shoes and a headband, sure I could get away with that - but not shoeless and shirtless in a pair of worn and dirty jeans. That would just be begging some flatfoot beat cop or patrol car to stop me. At least my bullet wound was covered now, but still, being noticed even that much would not be a good thing.

I needed to get some sort of vehicular transportation back up to Mid-Town.

The morning rush hour crowd was starting to fill out, and it would now be more difficult for me to elude detection. At a diner that already had a line-up down the street, I walked over to the a-frame style street sign and hefted it up and over my shoulders, wearing it like a sandwich board.

I started calling out "Eat at Charlie's Diner" in a monotone voice, and kept walking down the street and around the next block. Sure enough, the faces started to pay no attention to me.

Good old New Yorkers. All you needed to do to get people to ignore you was to try to get their attention.

God, I loved this city.

Another flash of memory from the night before struck me at that point. *The low howl of a siren as the scenery quickly flashed by in a blur. I was running, chasing another four-legged creature that was moving as fast as I could move. The scent ahead of me was confusingly much like the scent of another wolf, which made no sense.*

I shook my head and tried to drudge the memory back again.

All that returned was *the blur of the alley walls as I rushed past them and the two-toned whine of the approaching police siren.*

I'd made it about three blocks in this fashion when I finally encountered the scent of someone who seemed intrigued by the sign I was wearing. What I mean is that the curious nature was obvious, but there was a lingering scent of another emotion - desire.

Basically, somebody who'd spotted me wanted this sign for themselves.

I started panning the faces of the people nearby. Across the street and about half a block ahead of me sitting on the curb was an older woman in a long trench coat and faded green slacks. Mingled with her emotive scents was the smell of stale sweat and recent flatulence. Spotting her, I smiled and carefully crossed the street.

She held onto the shopping cart beside her - strategically stacked with an assortment of odds and ends several feet higher than the metal cage sides - with a firm clutching grip. It was apparent that you wouldn't be able to pry her fingers from that cart until she had been dead for several minutes.

She stood as I got within a few feet of her, still not letting go of her cart and grinned a wry, gap toothed smile at me.

"Nice sign, Cookie." She cackled with a bit of a slur. Fortunately for her, she'd been able to score some alcohol recently. After gaining my special sensory abilities, I was better able to understand others whose perceptions I couldn't quite grasp before. I found myself doing a lot less judging of people now, and simply accepted people for who they were. And, if alcohol helped her cope with the stress of what her day and her life was, then so be it.

"Thanks," I said, able to immediately detect that she was in a mood for bartering. As I stood close to her, it was a bit more difficult to filter out her vodka breath, the sour-milk body odor smell and get through to her emotive scents. "Care to make a trade?"

Her grin spread and she took her right hand off of her cart momentarily to run her palms together before clutching it once more.

"You don't happen to have a shirt my size in that cart of yours, do you?" I smiled.

She paused and glanced at the cart, her head tilting to one side. I could smell that she did have what I was looking for. "I might," she said. "What else you got."

"C'mon, lady." I said, throwing my arms up with my palms out. "Look at what I'm wearing here. I've got nothing but this sign and my pants."

"Not sure if that's a good deal for me, Cookie" she mused, but I could tell she was bluffing. It was as obvious to me as the fact that she'd just released a silent, but foul packet of flatulence into her pants. She still desperately wanted my sign.

"Fine," I said, starting to turn around. "See you later."

I made it about three steps, all the while smelling her anxiety growing exponentially.

"Wait a minute, Cookie! Wait a minute!"

~

Five minutes later I was walking away from our transaction wearing a slightly torn dress shirt that was a size too large for me and missing two buttons as well as a pair of mismatched shoes, one of which was a perfectly fitting sandal, the other was a sneaker that was a size too large, but with a torn sock stuffed in front of my toes, it fit okay.

Getting there, I told myself, and thought about Mack waiting for me at the Metro Market. I briefly considered my next step. Perhaps it should be to get a quarter so I could make a phone call to his cell phone and let him know that I was running late. But that thought was quickly dismissed given how I knew he detested such dalliances. Mack had the patience of a toddler and, despite the fact that I was now making him some pretty decent money, he wouldn't put up with a client that made him wait a single minute for an appointment. In his point of view, if a client couldn't be bothered to be on time for a meeting, he wouldn't waste another second working on their behalf.

I realized I was very fortunate to have found an agent like Mack, and while I'd be able to get another agent without issue, I found myself needing him - not just for business reasons, but for personal ones as well. Like Buddy, he was quirky but interesting, and he constantly challenged me. I found myself needing to be challenged in my personal relationships - if you didn't have to work hard at something, it almost didn't seem worth it.

And I definitely had to work hard to be in Mack's good books.

And that's where I wanted to stay.

I moved to Murray Street towards the subway entrance. I figured I'd be able to sneak onto the subway, but only with the additional thought that the next time I took the subway, I'd pay double to make up for my free ride.

Sure, a lot of people would make fun of me for trying to live my life so straight. But the person who I had to please most was myself, and, in the same way that Mack was true to himself, I set my own personal standards high for a good reason. After all, I was the one who had to live with the consequences of my actions.

And having blackouts of my time as a wolf was the hardest thing to deal with, particularly after waking up the way I had this morning. I mean, if I'd hurt an innocent person, or even worse, killed someone, I'm not sure how I'd be able to live with that.

A foggy string of memory from last night filtered up to my conscious mind. This time, the memory was completely non-visual, but I could tell I was *moving fast through an alley from the rapid patter of my paws on the pavement. I was chasing the wolf ahead of me. And, mingled with his hot breath was the distinct scent of human blood* - the same human blood that I woke up tasting.

A blaring horn to my immediate left broke the wispy memory. I glared at the driver as I continued walking towards the subway entrance.

So, there was another wolf.

What was I doing chasing him?

Yes, him, I knew it was a 'him' from the memory of his scent. That and the stink of human mingling with the canine scent meant that, like me, he was a werewolf. What else did I know? He had the blood on him that I'd tasted when I woke up.

This was getting curiouser and curiouser.

I moved down the stairs, starting to mesh in with the morning rush hour hustle, and, in the midst of the crowd, I was easily able to check for observant eyes and hop over the turnstile and make my way, virtually un-noticed except by a few people who'd been immediately behind me, down to the lower platform level. I shuffled through the crowd over to the far left of the platform, to ensure I "lost" the people who'd spotted me, just in case.

The rumbling of an approaching northbound train could be heard down the tunnel - this was good - I'd be able to make good time and get back to the hotel with enough time to get inside, have a quick shower, change, then be downstairs and around the block to meet Mack.

That's when I heard the faint gasp and brief cry for help amidst a scuffling.

I glanced at the approaching light of the train, then swiveled my head around, looking down the platform where I'd heard the cry come from. There was a balding middle-aged man in a grey suit surrounded by three goons all dressed in the same blue jeans, black t-shirts and red bandanas. They were either part of some gang, all had the same fashion consultant, or spent so much of their time stealing and vandalizing that they didn't give much time or thought to their own personal style. I was betting on the latter.

A glint of light from the blade of one of the men caught my eye as he waved his weapon, saying "I said, hand it over now."

The other two men flanked the bald man, each holding him by the upper arm.

"Aw crap," I mumbled, moving down the platform towards them - I was going to miss my train for sure.

"Hey!" I called out as I started rushing toward the melee. Behind me, the train arrived at the station.

The leader immediately turned to face me, bringing his knife in my direction as well. His lackeys also turned their attention toward me, which achieved the first of my goals.

I continued rushing the leader, and, just as I got within striking distance, he thrust the blade at me. I easily dodged the blade and him with a full body tackle, my left elbow raised to connect with his face.

His nose crunched noisily, and he actually caught a bit of air, trailing behind a thin stream of blood from his nose. His head connected with the wall first, his head making a satisfying hollow bong sound against the tile before he crumpled to the floor. I kicked the knife he'd dropped down to the track level just as the train started to pull out. Blocking the noise of the train, I focused on the sound of his heartbeat. It was still strong and steady; he was unconscious and relatively healthy, despite the smashed nose and bruised noggin.

The lackey on the man's left let go of his prey and rushed me while I was partially turned away. Given the setup, I could have easily used his momentum to flip him over my back and send him sprawling to the track level. But my goal wasn't to kill, merely to subdue.

Yes, I behaved more like a wolf and less like human every day.

I ducked under his rush, sending a right jab into his gut. My punch easily lifted him off of the ground, breaking a couple of ribs and knocking the breath out of him. As his feet came back onto the ground, I shoved him in the direction of his buddy and he stumbled, as if drunk, in a forward run, trying, vainly, to get his balance.

The buddy pushed his captive forward and ducked to the side. The man in the grey suit let out a moan as he collided with the incoming body, and he and the second goon piled to the floor in a mass of limbs.

I easily vaulted over the two, who lay there like lovers having just finished their business, grabbed the third attacker - who tried vainly to avoid my grasp by the scruff of his collar and slammed him, headfirst into the wall. He went down like last call at a frat bar.

At that point I offered a hand to the man in the grey suit who was now starting to catch his breath from the hit he had taken. He took my hand and I helped him to his feet

"T-thanks," he said, his eyes darting back and forth between the man he had just been laying in a pile on the floor with and the two who lay sprawled on the floor against the wall, as if nervous that they'd be getting up.

"Don't worry," I said. "They won't be going anywhere any time soon."

He looked over at me, as if seeing me for the first time, and did a double take. I wondered if he might be a fan of mine, recognizing who I really was, as he stood there, staring at me, his mouth agape.

Then he stepped forward, his voice low and gentle. "Listen. I'd like to thank you for helping me out."

"My pleasure," I said. I glanced around. Most of the morning commuters that had been on the platform with us had boarded the last train. However, a few people who'd gotten off this train and more people coming in from the street were milling around, just a few steps away, curiously looking at us and the unconscious men. I was eager for the next train to arrive and whisk me away from here.

"No, I mean it," he said, reaching in his back pocket and producing his wallet. He quickly thumbed it open and produced a twenty dollar bill. "Here. Maybe you can get yourself a warm meal."

I couldn't believe it. He thought I was a homeless person. But I couldn't blame him; after all, look at how I was dressed, how I smelled.

Dumbfounded, I tried to protest. "No, you don't need to …"

"Please, it's the least I can do," he said, pulling out another twenty.

Just then, a commotion started near the stairs. Oh shit. Security. I couldn't afford to be held back answering questions about the scuffle. It looked like I wouldn't be taking the next train after all. Damn.

"Thanks," I mumbled, sheepishly taking the forty dollars. I started to walk away quickly. "The guards are coming now. You'll be safe."

I tried to blend into the nearest crowd. It didn't work so well because many people cleared a wide path for me. These must have been people who'd seen the commotion. As I got deeper into the crowd, though, fewer people moved out of my way, and I squeezed my way through them, making a wide birth of the stairs as two security guards rushed toward my friend in the grey suit.

Continuing to move against the incoming crowd, I made my way up the stairs and to the street. For good measure I ran at top speed for several blocks.

As I ran, my mind flashed back to running in the alley again.

Racing low through the dark alley, the wolf ahead of me, its scent, and the blood of the human mingled with it enticing me to run faster. Finally, approaching the end of the alley as it met a street, I tensed and lunged into the air, coming down with my fangs just shy of the other wolf's neck. We rolled and he broke free, turned and faced me. My next nip was at his mouth, and my taste buds were infused with the human blood that coated his tongue and maw.

I continued walking north and was able to hail a cab by the time I reached Canal Street.

"The Algonquin Hotel," I said, climbing into the back of the taxi. "There's a twenty-dollar tip in it for you if you can get there within half an hour."

"No prob," the driver said, a wry grin on his face. "This car can find streets that aren't on anyone else's map."

I wasn't sure exactly what that meant, but his comment did fill me with confidence.

As the cab raced up Broadway and turned right on Grand, I sat back in the seat and rested my head, realizing it was the first time I'd stopped since waking up.

I closed my eyes and tried to conjure up more memories from last night, but none came, just this low throbbing sensation behind my eyes. I should know better than to try to force the memories.

When I opened my eyes, I saw there was a newspaper from the customer before me. New York Press. The large bold font headline read: "Vicious Wolf Attack Kills Man." The story mentioned a "pack of wolves" spotted running from the bloody scene where a homeless man was slaughtered. Police encountered the wolves near Fulton and Water, where shots were fired.

An officer claims to have wounded at least one of the wolves, but the animals quickly fled the scene and have yet to turn up elsewhere. One witness commented that "it was as if the streets just swallowed them up."

Midway through the article I must have faded off, because the next thing I knew the cabbie was telling me we had arrived. It made sense that I was overtired since I didn't actually spend last night sleeping, but rather running through the city streets, attacking another wolf, and being shot at by the police. No, not just shot at, but actually shot. And, since this had been the first time I'd sat down all morning, my body, overcome with fatigue, did the natural thing.

Out of habit I glanced at my wrist, but there was no watch there.

"I got you here in just under twenty minutes." The cabbie said, shaking his head, his eyes closed and wreaking of a deep, deep pride. "Man, they said it couldn't be done. But every day, every single day, I prove them wrong."

"Much to my satisfaction," I said, handing him the two twenties and stepping out of the cab.

As he pulled away, I realized I didn't have time to go inside, shower and get a change of clothes. I glanced at my reflection in the window of a van parked on the street. Okay, so I looked a little worse for wear. But I'd rather show up completely naked and with a giant turd on my head than to be late for a meeting with Mack.

As it was, once I walked down the street and around the block, I'd be just a few minutes early for our meeting, and that would be cutting it close enough.

Moving down the street, the sun now peeking through a break in the overcast sky, there was a slight spring in my step as I thought about what I would order for breakfast. At that thought my stomach growled.

In the back of my mind, I wondered when I might again meet that other wolf who was stalking in my territory. It was a mystery I'd likely solve some other time around, but at the thought of that other wolf, I growled.

It was a softer, quieter growl than the one my stomach had just made.

About the Story

"THIS TIME AROUND" was a short story originally written for a werewolf themed anthology. I was trying to write a story that demonstrated what it might be like to live with the side-effect of being a werewolf, without actually having the wolf appear in the tale. This story never made the cut, but there was something about the character of Michael Andrews that really stuck with me. So, I kept refining the story.

When, Sean Costello, a mentor and fellow writer read the story, the first thing he said to me was: "This is great! What happens next?"

"What do you mean" I asked him. "Nothing happens next. That's the end of the story."

"No, it's not the end of the story," he grinned. "It's the beginning of a novel."

I put a lot of thought into his words and realized that, even though I had intended the story to end there, there was something unresolved about the main character's day. I never did get into the mystery of that other wolf. I just thought it might be something intriguing for the reader to wonder about.

But as I explored that unresolved element I had planted, I began to wonder about who the other werewolf was and whether or not Michael would actually encounter him. I wondered a lot more about Michael's double-life, and about what sorts of relationships he might have because of that.

And I began to adapt this story into a novel entitled **A Canadian Werewolf in New York**. Based on working with an amazing editor, Joshua Essoe, I spent a significant amount of time revising the novel, which was released in it's first incarnation, in December 2016.

I have since gone on to write another novella in what I'm calling the *Canadian Werewolf* universe and, as I write this, am at work on a further short story and the second full length novel, which will be called *Fear and Longing in Los Angeles*.

But, if you like this story, and the character of my narrator, Michael Andrews, then I suspect you might enjoy the full-length novel **A Canadian Werewolf in New York**, which is available in eBook, print (trade paperback and hardcover editions), and audiobook.

Where this story outlines the early morning of Michael's day, the novel covers the entire day; or, at least the part of the day where he is a man, with brief interludes of those moments when he is a wolf, which help slowly unravel the mystery of what happened the night before.

If you do end up picking up the novel, please note that the first five chapters of the book loosely overlap with the early AM events which are documented in this story. It has Michael waking up in Battery Park and the rush to get to his morning meeting with his agent. Those opening moments were re-adapted into a prologue to explain Michael's back-story a bit, and a series of chapters, as well as a couple of interludes entitled "Wolf Night." And, while the details of what happens to Michael in the early morning hours remains the same, there are differences to the phrases, the dialogue, as well as additional character development and other window-dressing pieces, based on the differences of writing and editing for a longer work versus a short story.

The novel, of course, goes on to explore what happens once he arrives at his breakfast meeting as well as for the remainder of Michael's day. Here is the synopsis for the novel:

Writer. Werewolf. Canadian.

Michael Andrews seems to have it all. He's a successful author and a minor celebrity living in Manhattan. It's a pretty big step up from his humble Canadian upbringing. Of course, his lycanthropy poses a bit of a challenge. After waking up from his latest night on the town, he's naked, he's got a bullet hole in his leg, and he has a sneaking suspicion he ran into another wolf last night.

If he's going to make an evening talk show appearance to promote his latest book, he'll need to figure out what happened the previous night without letting his occasional heroics get in the way. Standing in his way are an agent, an ex-girlfriend, a variety of goons, and a fellow wolf encroaching on his territory.

It's just another day in the life of a polite, small-town Canadian trying to stay alive in the Big Apple.

A Canadian Werewolf in New York is a humorous thriller about an ordinary man dealing with extraordinary circumstances. If you like seeing an everyman try to "do right" no matter the odds, then you'll love this suspenseful and comedic tale of a Canadian bumpkin who happens to be part wolf.

To potentially satisfy your "sneak peek" pleasure, the next page contains the opening of Chapter Six; basically, what immediately follows the moment where Michael is about to enter the diner and hears his stomach growl.

Enjoy!

Mark Leslie
July 2020

ACWWINY Sneak Peek at Chapter Six: A red-letter breakfast with Mack the Knife

"YOU LOOK LIKE a bag of shit."

I couldn't help but smile at Mack. Being greeted in such a way immediately told me that I wasn't in his bad books.

Mack had a wry smile on his face as he looked up at me, his thin lips pressed tightly beneath an even thinner, dark mustache that looked more like it was drawn on than grown. I'd always thought that with his thick, brush-cut hair, dark around the ears, but blending into a soft grey at the top, he'd look better in a fuller, thicker moustache. But I kept telling myself that would make him look more like the J. Jonah Jamieson from the Spider-Man comic books.

I felt a huge knot of tension release in my shoulders and I let the glorious smells of various breakfast foods in the open-kitchen restaurant wash over me.

"What did you do?" Mack said, still sitting at the table and grinning at me as I approached. "Sleep on the street last night?"

"Good morning Mack." I tried to ignore his insult and move on. "So, can we order food now?"

But he wasn't finished.

"You decide to roll naked in a garbage dumpster before meeting me this morning?"

"Mack, I'm a little peckish this morning."

"What, you couldn't find something good to eat in the dumpster? Man, but you artistic types – you never cease to surprise me with the way you dress in public." He clasped his hands together while I sat, revealing that he was finished with his fun and ready to get down to business. "I already ordered for both of us. They're cooking it now."

Of course he would have. He'd never expect one of his clients to be late, or this was the last meeting he'd have with them. Smiling again, I pulled out the chair across from him and sat.

"Promise me something," Mack said.

I nodded. "Sure."

"Promise me you've got something else to wear for tonight's spot on Letterman."

I just looked at him. Did he just say *Letterman*?

"You heard me, didn't you?"

I nodded again. *Letterman*? *David* freaking *Letterman*?

"I got the call last night. They had another writer scheduled to appear on the show. One of those self-help guru types, Andy Robinson, I think. It was a last minute cancellation. So, a phone call or two later and voila, Michael Andrews is on."

I was still at a loss for words. Letterman? I kept repeating to myself. I knew there was a reason I put up with Mack's insults and gruff nature. It was because he could pull something like this off.

"I'd been trying to get you on the show for the past year and the producers must have had you front of mind. But you have to admit, the timing couldn't be better."

My last novel, *Print of the Predator*, had been released about four months ago, but a collection of my short fiction was due out in a few weeks. Mack and my publisher had been pushing me for the past couple of years to release something to keep my fans sated between the standard annual spring releases of my novels.

I was eager to see reader reaction to a collection of the more morbid writings reflective of my earlier years as a writer – the collection was a compilation of stories that had originally appeared in small press magazines years before my name became known alongside a few newer tales I had penned in the same macabre style.

And I'd be appearing on the Letterman show, just weeks before the book's release. Is there any wonder why I was desperate to hang onto Mack as my agent?

"Letterman?" I finally said, as our breakfast arrived, two steaming plates of eggs, hash browns, ham, bacon and sausage. A plate with a single stack of half a dozen pieces of toast sat in the middle of the tray beside two tall glasses of orange juice, two glasses of milk and a large coffee for me. Another thing about hanging around with Mack – known in literary circles as "Mack the Knife" for his ability to get what he desired – were the fringe benefits of being in his presence. This Metro Market didn't serve food to tables. Despite their ability to cook virtually anything your heart desired it was standard counter service. You ordered at the counter, paid up front, and carried the food on trays to your table. But not with Mack. No matter where he was or what he wanted, I've yet to see him be denied a request.

Gotta love that he's my agent.

While I squeezed the ketchup onto my plate, Mack started shaking salt onto his own, as if he were trying to bleed the shaker dry. "You'll be appearing," he said, "alongside the hot new shock-rock dude. Knell. I'm rather fond of that concept, because it might open you up to a whole new audience. Given the likely attention span of his fans, it's perfect that you're promoting your book of short stories." He turned his attention to the pepper, shaking as vigorously as he had with the salt. "You should try to work in a mention of the story about the serial killer who takes out concert groupies – that oughta get their attention."

I could only nod enthusiastically at that point, because I'd already stuffed several forkfuls of food into my mouth.

Knell was definitely the latest hot commodity with young folks. A young, blond rock star with a perpetual Billy Idol sneer, he came off like a cross between Eminem and Ozzy Osbourne. His music was raunchy and hard hitting, and his lyrics rolled off his tongue like he'd just chugged a cocktail of laxatives and hard liquor.

His lyrics were controversial, his band a group of talented musicians, and he was splashed all over the media, pushing Kim Kardashian from the top spot of those celebrities the average person just loved to hate. If it wasn't a story about his songs being banned from school dances, it was a tale about his raunchy night club escapades.

Yet, his albums were an interesting compilation, because both of them contained not only the hard-hitting songs with lyrics that pushed the envelope of taste and decency but there were also at least two tracks that were clean enough for standard radio airplay. That's how I'd heard most of his music. I'd also overheard some of the raunchier songs from personal mp3 players while on public transit – and you wouldn't need my heightened sense of sound to pick up on those, let me tell you. I started reminding myself of my father lately, thinking that the hearing-aid industry would likely be booming due to the volume with which young people blasted tunes into their heads.

Mack was right. It would be interesting to see if my appearance with Knell could capture a new type of audience.

"Woah, slow down, there, Chester," Mack said, taking a mouthful of juice. "I don't plan on taking any of that food away from you. I've got my own."

I just glared at him, shoveling another couple of mouthfuls in. Now that I'd gotten a taste of the food, I was almost not able to meet the demands of my stomach and bring the food in fast enough.

"Oh wait," he said, pointing at my plate. "I know what it is. You've got so much ketchup on your plate, you can't even see the food." He took another chug of his juice and grinned. "You're panicked – trying to ensure that there is food under all that ketchup."

I thought it was funny that he'd make so much fun of me after he'd almost depleted the salt and pepper shakers over his own plate. But Mack was like that. If we were both sitting there with bird-shit in our hair, he'd be laughing his ass off at my predicament, completely unaware that he looked just as silly.

"Okay," the tone in his voice took on a seriousness that I could also smell. "One more business item to discuss so I can properly claim this meal as a business expense. Your publisher called yesterday and they want to see progress on the next Maxwell Bronte novel. They want to see the first five thousand words or so to ensure it's coming along. I've held them off as long as possible, but you gotta start producing."

Maxwell Bronte was the hero in my mystery novels. He worked in antiquities and usually solved mysteries in the world of books and antiques. It was a good series, and Maxwell was a fun character to explore, but after six novels, two of which had been turned into movies, one a feature length film and the other a made-for-television special that doubled as a pilot for a television series that never went anywhere, I wanted to explore other things in my writing.

I guess I was experiencing what sometimes happens to writers who create a character who is both interesting, marketable and successful. A Frankenstein monster of my own that I couldn't escape from.

That's another reason why I liked the fact that my short-story collection would be coming out – it would be good to attract some new readers, readers who might not already be familiar with Maxwell Bronte, readers who enjoyed the dark and twisted turns my stories could take, and didn't want just another antiquity mystery.

In the meantime, my contract stipulated that I had to produce three more Maxwell Bronte novels in the next three years. Maybe after that I could explore other writing.

The problem, recently, had been that while I had been writing, I hadn't done much on the latest Maxwell Bronte novel. All my writing had either been short-story diversions, or notes towards a few supernatural thrillers. I'd even started a series of humorous essays outlining what it was like to be a Canadian born in a Northern Ontario town and living in Manhattan.

Maxwell Bronte was currently an elusive character for me lately, just outside the range of my creative spark. Sure, I'd been with him on some great adventures, but neither my mind nor my pen had been able to track him down and capture what he was up to.

I hadn't let Mack know any of that, of course, because every time I mentioned working on other writing projects, he pointed out the contract – which had paid quite. He'd only let the release of the short stories through because one of the tales included a mention of Bronte as a young man. Mack saw this as a wonderful teaser, and was ensuring – against my wishes – that the publisher included a qualifier on the cover indicating a Maxwell Bronte adventure appeared in the book.

So while the short story collection might attract a new audience and increase my readership, the insertion of Maxwell Bronte into one of the tales and in the promotions for the book guaranteed that the regular Bronte fans would rush to the stores to buy it, just for another simple taste of their favorite character.

In the back of my mind, I knew it was likely that many of these fans would buy the book and only read the tale with Bronte in it, overlooking the rest.

That hurt. I know, I should be thankful that my books are selling at all – hell, that they're even being published. But I needed more as a writer than just a fan base waiting for the next in a seemingly endless mystery series.

I needed to explore the human condition in so many other ways than a single character's exploits could take me – sure, there were supporting characters and new people who moved in and out of Bronte's life. But I never got a chance to simply follow one of them along and see where their story took me.

The blur of graffiti from the alley walls as I rushed past them, the echo of the high-low wail of a siren, and ahead of me, maintaining its lead, another wolf.

The sudden flashback didn't take me by surprise, they rarely did any more, but when I have them, I do pause, my eyes go glassy, and I sometimes lose track of the conversation. At times both Max and a now ex-girlfriend used to suggest I go for a brain scan to see if perhaps I suffered from a mild form of epilepsy. Max was in the middle of saying something when I was able to again focus on the conversation.

". . . remind you that you're under contract and already two months behind schedule," he was saying. "And mostly because they and I allowed you a small grace period so you could get that little short story collection worked out of your system."

I stabbed the last few hash browns and glanced back up at Mack. "I'll have something to you by the end of the week," I said around a mouthful.

"No," Mack said.

His words, eyes, and his scent were like a face-full of cold water thrown in my face. He had a way of inserting his entire being into a statement, a moment. His heart even paused and beat a single strong pulse at the exact right time, as if offering an exclamation point to his word. I know that my heightened senses picked up on many of these things, but I was convinced that they also came across, quite clearly to the average person when Mack spoke.

"You'll have me five thousand words by the time you're ready to be on Letterman tonight."

"But Mack . . ."

"Don't hand me that bull, Andrews. This is a walk in the freakin' park for you. You can shit out five hundred perfectly crafted words by the time it takes me to finish my breakfast. You've got the entire day. What else is on your schedule?" He paused, then added with a bemused smirk. "Besides perhaps a much-needed shower and wardrobe change?"

I thought about that other werewolf, about trying to unravel what had happened to my alter ego the night before, about the murder, about the shooting.

"Nothing," I said.

"Don't give me that – I can see in your eyes that you've got these big plans. What are you doing, working on those non-Bronte pieces? Dammit, Michael, haven't I come through for you on all angles? For at least one year I had to put up with you jumping around, a strained look on your face as you gestured for me to pull your damn finger so you could get this fart that had been building in your system out. Well, I pulled your damn finger – relieved you of that fart. Can't you at least do me the favor of getting your ass in front of your computer and pounding out five thousand simple words in the next Bronte adventure?"

"Fine," I said.

The conversation was over at that point. Sure, there were small words to be exchanged, the bill to be paid. But it was over. Mack's heartbeat suddenly relaxed, his mood shifted from work back to relaxation. He'd stated his case, won. Victory was his, and he wasted no time enjoying it.

"Two o'clock," his words weren't punctuated with the sudden single throb of his heart. This was merely a casual add-on for him to a lifetime of bargaining and winning. No matter what he won, what he got, he always pushed for more. It was like breathing to him I guess.

I glanced over at a clock on the wall. It was 7:50 a.m. By the time I got to my place and showered, I'd likely have about five and a half hours.

This Time Around

It was only five thousand words after all. I had to stop being a big baby about it. Five thousand words was nothing – a couple of hours work perhaps.

"Fine," I said again.

Mack struck a match against the flat, plastic no-smoking placard attached to the surface of the table and smiled at me as he lit a cigar.

About the Author

MARK LESLIE is a writer, editor and bookseller who was born and grew up in Sudbury, Ontario, spent many years in Ottawa and Hamilton, Ontario and currently lives in Waterloo, Ontario.

When he's not writing, Mark attaches "Lefebvre" back onto his name and works as a writing and publishing coach and consultant. As Director of Self-Publishing and Author Relations for Rakuten Kobo between 2011 and 2017, Mark established Kobo Writing Life which represents between 10 and 18% of Kobo's weekly unit sales, larger than any of the major publishers.

A bookselling veteran for more than twenty years, Mark has worked at virtually every type of bookstore, has sat on the Board of Directors for BookNet Canada and also been President of the Canadian Booksellers Association. He has given talks across Canada and the United States, in London, Paris and Frankfurt on the bookselling, writing and publishing industry.

Mark can be found online at www.markleslie.ca.

Selected Works

Non-fiction paranormal:

- *Haunted Hamilton: The Ghosts of Dundurn Castle and Other Steeltown Shivers* (2012)
- *Spooky Sudbury: True Tales of the Eerie & Supernatural* (2013) – Co-written with Jenny Jelen
- *Tomes of Terror: Haunted Bookstores and Libraries* (2014)
- *Creepy Capital: Ghost Stories of Ottawa and the National Capital Region* (2016)
- *Haunted Hospitals: Eerie Tales about Hospitals, Sanatoriums and Other Institutions* (2017) – Co-written with Rhonda Parrish
- *Macabre Montreal: Ghostly Tales, Ghastly Events, and Gruesome True Stories* (2018) – Co-written with Shayna Krishnasamy

Fiction:

- *One Hand Screaming* (2004)
- *Evasion* (2014)
- *I, Death* (2016)
- *A Canadian Werewolf in New York* (2016)
- *Nocturnal Screams* (Short Fiction Series) (2017/2018)
- *Stowe Away* (2020)

Editor:

- *North of Infinity II* (2006)
- *Campus Chills* (2009)
- *Tesseracts Sixteen: Parnassus Unbound* (2012)
- *Fiction River 23: Editors' Choice* (2017)
- *Fiction River 25: Feel the Fear* (2017)
- *Fiction River 31: Feel the Love* (2019)
- *Fiction River 32: Superstitious* (2019)

www.ingramcontent.com/pod-product-compliance
Lightning Source LLC
Chambersburg PA
CBHW020648130626
46552CB00003B/1453